CONFESSIONS

CONFESSIONS
VOLUME 1

A collection of erotic confessions

Selected and edited by Miranda Forbes

Published by Accent Press Ltd – 2009
ISBN 9781907016318

Copyright © Accent Press Ltd 2009

Printed and bound in the UK

Cover design by
Red Dot Design

Contents

MIKE — Lowestoft

2

The Secret Place

I know I shouldn't have followed her, and maybe I shouldn't even have been looking but what can a guy do? She just looked so good, with her little round bum cheeks moving in her bikini pants. You know how it is, when the bit at the back hardly covers the girl's bum and the material is just a little bit loose, so you can see her shape and quite a lot of bum cheeks but it's as big a tease as it is a show. Hers was blue, and it looked so hot against her tanned skin, with her dark blonde hair and her shades pushed up onto her forehead. Oh yeah, and she had no top on, only her back was to me.

That's why I followed her. I told myself I'd just walk along the beach a bit, not too close or anything, and once I'd got past her I'd turn around, like I'd left something in the car or something. That way I'd get to have a nice, long look at her tits without her realising I was

3

staring. That was the idea anyway, but it didn't work out like that. I got my look, and she was everything I'd hoped for, little firm titties with dark nipples sticking up like puppy dog's noses, so fucking cute I could have died. She had a serious case of cameltoe going on too, and I could tell she was shaved, 'cause the front of her bikini clung to the V shape between her legs like it had been painted on.

Maybe I should have just gone up into the dunes and found somewhere quiet to jack off, but the back of this beach, in Suffolk, near where I live, is full in summer of gay guys cruising and I didn't want any of them to get the wrong idea. She wasn't taking any notice of anyway, like she was in another world, just walking along the beach, cool as a cucumber with that darling little bum going up and down in her bikini pants. So I followed, far enough behind so she wouldn't freak out, and wondering why a girl who obviously didn't mind getting her tits out on the beach wanted to go so far along. When I first saw her we were maybe half a mile from the car park, and she just kept on going. I thought maybe she was going to go nude, and I wanted an eyeful of that like I couldn't stop myself.

I did thinking about trying to get talking to her, but it wasn't going to work. She was maybe half my age, a young 44 if you want to know, and just so cool and classy. Not that I'm that bad, but I could guess the sort of answer I'd get if I came on to her, so it was better to keep quiet and watch. I didn't want her to even notice me, so I hung back a bit more, until I was a long way behind her. She just kept on, not even looking back at first, then starting to look over her shoulder every so often like she was checking nobody was following her.

I thought she'd seen me, so I stopped and sat down. I was telling myself I'd had my kicks and ought to head back, only she'd got my interest up in more ways than one, if you get what I mean, so I was going to have to cool off a bit or maybe get arrested. I went in the sea, just up to my middle, and that worked, only when I turned around again she was gone. That was weird, because the beach is dead straight for miles and she hadn't come back and she wasn't in the sea. She had to have gone up into the dunes, and that had to mean she was going to go nude.

I could just see it. We were well past where the gays hang out, so she'd be on her own, maybe in some little sandy hollow out of the wind. She'd kneel down and get her stuff out of the bag she'd got, a mag maybe and some lotion. She'd be a bit shy at first, wanting to make sure she was really alone, and she'd just sit there, rubbing the lotion into her arms and legs and neck, then her titties. God I wanted to watch that, her creamy fingers rubbing over those two sweet little mounds, making them jiggle and perking up those little brown nipples even harder than they'd been when I saw them. That would get her going, and off would come those little blue bikini pants, to show off her bum, and more.

I really did try not to do it, but I found myself walking towards the place where I reckoned she'd gone in. There was nobody else about, not within a long way, only a few people far off along the beach. I tried to look casual, like I just happened to be walking through the dunes, but I knew if she saw me she'd know. That's why I went slowly, checking everything out before I got any further, only she just wasn't there.

I couldn't figure it out at all. She'd gone in the dunes, she had to have, but when I climbed up the back I could see into all the hollows and she wasn't there. The only place I couldn't see was this little sort of wood with silvery grey trees, but there wasn't going to be a lot of sun there. I'd lost her, and I felt so fucking frustrated. You can imagine. I just had to jack off, but I didn't want to risk getting caught, so I went right up to the top of the dunes and sat down where this little path went through. I could see all around, but the most anyone could see of me would be my head poking up in the grass, and that only if they were looking.

I was just about to get the old man out when I saw something, somebody's head, just bobbing up for a moment. At first I thought it might be her, or some gay guy come a bit further than usual, but then she pops up again. It was another girl, maybe not quite so fit as my babe in the blue bikini and still with her kit on, but good. She was coming towards me too, and I was praying she would choose one of the hollows I could see into and strip off where I could watch.

What she did was walk into the little wood.

I didn't know what she was up to, but I was pretty sure it was something private. That made me think twice, and I did tell myself I ought to leave her in peace, but my cock was telling me different. I stayed where I was for a bit, feeling guilty but horny too, before deciding that it wouldn't hurt if I took a little peep, just to see what they were up to. You see, I love looking at girls, but it's a much bigger kick if they don't know they're being watched, or if they give a bit of a show by accident. I'd rather see a girl in a bikini just walking on the beach, or even in tight jeans on the street than I would see the same girl do a full on strip in a bar. Where's the fun if you're allowed to see it?

Down I went, to the edge of the little wood and in, going really careful. It felt great, horny and daring too, and the wood was perfect, with little twisted trees and patches of thicker stuff so I could go along without risking being seen. It was really thick too, and I saw sunlight ahead of me before anything else, which told me there was an open space in the middle. There was too, one of the little hollows like you always get in sand dunes, only with trees all round so you couldn't see it at all, even from the top of the bigger dunes.

They were they, not just two girls, but three, my blonde babe, the one I'd watched arrive and another girl who must have come earlier, and just that first look nearly made me come in my pants. My blonde was laid out on a towel, stark fucking naked, face down, that sweet little bum she'd been showing off in her blue bikini pants bare and just as firm and round and perfect as I'd imagined. Next to her, side by side, was the girl who'd got there first. She was darker, with sort of olive-coloured skin, maybe Greek or something, a bit shorter but with curves like you've never see, huge titties squashed out under her chest and a bum like a ripe peach, all of it nude and with her legs just a little bit apart so I got a sneaky glimpse of rear view cameltoe. The third girl was the best, not because she was any cuter than her friends, but because she was just starting to undress.

She was completely casual about it, like she was on her own in her bedroom or something, and that was what made it so horny. They already had me hard, just looking at them, and when she unclips her bra like it just doesn't fucking matter one little bit, I had to unzip. Off comes her bra and out come two round little titties, not so little actually and do you know what she does? As they come out she cups them in her hands, like she's weighing them or something, or maybe checking them out to remind herself what she can do for the boys.

She did something for this one, I tell you. It was only 'cause I was hoping there'd be more to come that I didn't come in my hand, and if there's one thing I like better than a pair of bare titties it's a bare bum. She had a beauty too, filling out her jeans like they'd been spray painted on. She put her hands on the button and I swear I stopped breathing. The button comes open, down come her zip, her thumbs go in the sides and down it all comes, jeans and panties and all, with her bum stuck out just a little bit so as she goes bare I get to see the hole between her cheeks and just a flash of cunt.

That was it, too much. I'd come and I didn't even put it away before I got right out of there. My heart was going like a fucking jack hammer, I tell you, and I was sure they'd heard me. Nobody followed though and none of them came out of the wood. I'd got away with it.

That was the first time, and I could not stop thinking about what had happened. Fuck knows I've watched girls on beaches for years, and I've seen plenty, but I'd never got that lucky. I mean, three of them, not one you'd kick out of bed and all stark fucking naked. I wanted more, and I figured that the wood was somewhere they went quite a lot, like a secret place they could strip off completely and not be seen, not until I'd caught them at it anyway.

I had to go back, just to check, and I did. The next two times nobody was there, but I checked it out and I'd been right. They'd got it all nicely set up, with the path going in around the back of a bush and even some twigs and stuff to make it look like the path didn't go anywhere. You couldn't see the hollow until you were right on top of it, and you'd hear anybody coming unless they were really careful, like me.

The fourth time was good. When I arrived my sexy blonde was there on her own, reading a book in the nude. I took it a bit more easy this time, enjoying the show, and what a show. Without even her mates there she was even more easygoing about being naked, face down with her bum on show, on her back with her titties pointing up at the sky and legs a little apart to show off her cameltoe, but it was best when she turned over. She didn't just roll round, you see, she pulled herself up on her knees and tugged her towel out straight. That meant for one perfect moment she was on her knees, titties dangling down, bum up and her knees a little bit open so I could see everything, and I do mean everything. 'Cause she was skinny her cheeks were right open, showing off every fucking detail. Her bumhole was like a little star, bright pink and real tight, so I just wanted to stick my tongue right up it and then my cock. She had the most gorgeous cunt too, shaved and pink, ever so neat, like she was a virgin or something, although some lucky bastard had to have fucked her, 'cause she was just too good to miss.

The best thing was, she was regular, turning over every now and then like she thought she was a burger on a barbie. That nearly fucking killed me, watching her one way up or the other and knowing I only had to wait before she'd be back on her knees with that little arse on show again. Three times I watched her turn over and managed not to come, but the fourth time was too much. I felt like I was going to burst anyway, just with her lying there and her bum on show, but as she gets up to roll over a bit of sand must have got in the wrong place or something, cause this time when she sticks her bum up in the air she reaches back and gives her hole a little tickle, like she's got an itch, or maybe she's going to get horny with herself and stick a finger up. I came, and I swear if it went much further she'd have gotten wet.

After that I came every day I could. I couldn't get enough. I didn't care about anything else. Even if it looked like it was going to rain I'd be there, and of course they weren't, but I couldn't stand the thought of missing out. I'd get up early so I could be in place before they came, and after a while I stopped leaving when I'd come. I knew their routine, you see, where they'd come in and how they'd lie, and all the best places to make sure I got a good look but they'd never see me.

I'd get lucky maybe three times in five, 'cause they did like to go there and they always went nude. There were five in all, the three I'd seen the first time and two I reckon might have been sisters, 'cause they looked much the same and usually came together. I didn't know their names, then, and I only know one now, but after a couple of weeks they'd become as familiar to me as any girlfriend ever has, their bodies anyway. There was Blondie, the first and maybe the best, with her cool look and her sweet little bum. There was Shy, the Greek looking one, called that 'cause she had this funny way of getting all embarrassed when she undressed, using a towel and covering her titties with her arm, even though she didn't seem to mind sunbathing in the nude. Then there was Fudge, the one I'd spunked over when she took her jeans and panties down, called that 'cause she sometimes bought a box of clotted cream fudge with her. The last two were Big Sis and Little Sis, who were both blondes and not there that often.

When they were it was good, 'cause they

used to rub lotion into each others' back and stuff. Nothing dirty, of course, but just to see them take turns to do it was enough. They'd even do each others' bums and tits, and that was always too much for me. Big Sis was taller and a bit meatier, with plenty of everything, and to see her lifting up those big titties so Little Sis could get the lotion on evenly, I swear, that was enough to give a fucking statue a hard on.

I always used to hope they'd get into some lezzie action, not the sisters maybe, if they even were sisters, but some of the others. It just seemed such a good chance to get horny with each other, what with being in the nude and all oiled up and stuff. I think maybe Shy would have been into it, cause she was always a bit self-conscious about her body, but when the others undressed she used to watch. I used to imagine it, how maybe she'd offer to rub some lotion in for Blondie or Fudge, first her back and legs, then her bum, and all the while gradually getting more and more horny until in the end they got down to it, cuddling up on their towels for a good grope of each others bums and tits, then taking turns to lick pussy, or maybe going sixty-nine with their bums in each others' faces.

That never happened, but I did get to watch Fudge get herself off. It was a seriously hot day, right at the end of July. I'd been there since before any of the girls turned up, and I'd seen plenty already. I'd watched Blondie strip and get oiled up, and seen Fudge doing exercises that made her tits bounce and gave me a great show of cunt from behind. Maybe that's what got her horny, 'cause afterwards she seemed really restless, and when Blondie left I knew something was up. Normally they'd just say goodbye, even they didn't leave together, but this time Fudge said she'd follow on and stayed where she was, sitting up cross-legged and pretending to read a magazine. Blondie went and no sooner had she gone than Fudge jumps up and follows, like she's checking to make sure her mate has really gone. When she comes back she biting her lip, and she stops to listen for a bit. Then she lies down on her towel again, with her eyes shut and her hands on her tummy.

I thought maybe she was going to go to sleep, but oh no. After a bit her hands start to move, touching herself really gently, just her tummy at first, but then her tits and I knew what she was up to. I've seen girls get themselves off before, but usually to show off for me. This was different, like everything was concentrated on herself. It was still a good show though, with both hands on her titties at first, feeling them up and making her nipples hard, feeling their size too, like she had the first time. I reckon she had a thing about showing off her tits, and maybe she was thinking of her boyfriend or some bloke she fancied. Anyway, she spent ages just feeling herself, all the time with her eyes shut and her head to one side. I was keeping pace and I could have come easy, but like before I was sure there'd be more to come.

I was right. Her legs came up, and open, showing off her cunt like she expected some guy to get on top of her, which must have been what she was thinking about. She stayed like that for a bit, still playing with her titties, only then her hand goes down between her legs and she's doing it full on, getting herself off with one hand on her cunt and a tit in the other. I tell you, I nearly went down and joined in, only I knew she'd scream the place down and stayed as I was, both of us frigging away.

What she was showing was enough for me and I finished off in no time. She took ages, teasing herself and stopping every now and then to listen out, with her face in this big, sloppy smile, like she was so happy she couldn't stop grinning. Then her mouth starts to come open, a little bit at first, then wide and all of a sudden she's snatching at her pussy and pinching her nipple, real hard. She screamed out when she came, and her whole body was shaking, so it must have been a good one.

That's how I knew Fudge was the dirty one. Not that I planned to do anything, 'cause I knew if they caught me it would be all over, and girls hate guys who get off over them without them calling the shots, and yeah, I was being a dirty bastard. I did think about trying to meet one of them somewhere else, but it wouldn't have been the same, 'cause even if I got to be her boyfriend I knew I'd never be invited to their secret place, or if I was the others wouldn't want to go nude. It was best to watch, and I'd have been happy if it had stayed that way.

What happened was that Fudge caught me. Not peeping, but she wasn't just the dirty one, she was the clever one and all. I always tried to get there early, and take a long way around so they wouldn't figure out that I was always around, but she did. How, I don't know, but one day as I'm walking through the dunes she's waiting there, sitting on the grass in her bikini, just like butter wouldn't melt in her mouth.

Maybe I gave a start or something when I saw it was her, but she knew, 'cause she had this odd look on her face, like accusing but excited too. Then she comes right out with it. "Hello, you little pervert." Course I pretended I didn't know what she was talking about, but she tells me to shut up, then goes on. "I know you look at us sunbathing. I'll do you a deal. You stop it and never tell anybody about our place, and I'll –"

She made sign with her hand, like she was calling somebody a wanker. I knew what she meant, but I thought it was a trick or something, and when I got my cock out she'd scream rape. I didn't know what to say anyway, and just stood there like a prat, until

19

she got down to the path I was on. I just let her, and believe me, she was no innocent. She just pushed me back against the bank, made a quick check to make sure nobody was about, and unzipped me. Once she'd started to touch I wasn't going to stop her, because she really knew what she was doing. She got my balls out too, cupping them and weighing them just like she used to do with her tits, and wanking my cock at the same time.

I just took it all in. She'd gone down kneeling, and I love it when girls do that, with my cock right in front of my face as I started to get hard. She was horny about it too, not like some girls, but weird too, calling me a pervert and a dirty old man and saying things like "I bet you like to see my boobs, don't you, you dirty bastard" and sure enough, out they come, for me to look at and then are wrapped around my cock, so I'm titty fucking her while she's calling me a pervert and a filthy pig and every bastard under the sun. She really got off on it too. Before long she'd forgotten all about just tossing me off. She's got my cock in her mouth and she she's squeezing my balls like she's trying to milk me dry, only when I try to touch one of those gorgeous big tittles she slaps my hand. It was too late anyway, cause another second and I'd come in her mouth. She swallowed the lot, then looks up with this big smile and says "That's the deal. No peeking, but if you're here tomorrow, just maybe you'll get more." I was there tomorrow, which is when I learnt she was really called Becky, although nowadays I generally just call her the Mrs.

JERRY — Wolverhampton

Coming on Command

My thing is making girls come. Okay, so what? Most guys like to give their girls pleasure, but this is a bit different. I like to do it so they can't stop it happening, and best of all I like to do it in public.

I like it anyway, the way they just lose it and start to moan and scream, the way their thighs go tight and their pussies and bums squeeze, the way they lose control and start talking dirty or begging for my cock. It's all great, and I love to watch a girl masturbate or lick her until she makes it, or bring her off while I fuck her, but none of that is as good making her do it when she can't stop it happening and there are people around to watch.

The easiest way is to take a girl who likes to be told what to do out dogging. Sammy was like that, my little blonde. She got off on me

25

making her do stuff, and the ruder the better. We used to go out to dogging sites, out near the Essex coast, especially this one big car park where you might get as many as twenty, even thirty men and maybe five or six cars with action. I'd give the signal and put Sammy's seat down, then order her to kneel on it and stick her bum out towards the windscreen so everybody got a good view. I'd make her pull her top up to show her tits and leave it like that, maybe play with them for a bit, then push down her jeans and knickers at the back to show everybody her bum and pussy. That used to get to her like nothing else, because she loved to think of all the men seeing every single bit of her body, but my kick came from making her frig off in front of them, sometimes with her fingers, sometimes with this little silver vibrator she had, and sometimes I'd do it for her, but it was always all the way, until she'd come and they'd all seen. I especially liked the way her bumhole used to wink when she got there, and I even put that on video so she could see.

That was good, and I've done it with other girls too, but it's never the best because it's just in front of a load of dirty old wankers. They just lap it up, and the girls know they love it, so where's the edge? Better than that, which I've only done a couple of times, is to make a girlfriend masturbate at a party. Obviously you need somebody who's up for it, but the other people who're there don't need to know that. One time was with Sam and we'd set it all up with a group of mates. Sometimes we used to play strip poker, only normally it didn't go that far, maybe bare tits or a guy having to strip off, but not much more. This time we set it up carefully, with Sam bluffing a guy called Neil who reckoned himself when it came to poker. She wouldn't back down, and we both knew he wouldn't, so when all her money's in the middle of the table she starts offering forfeits, first her bra, then her panties, then to give him a lap dance, and at last to masturbate in front of all of us. She lost, just like we'd arranged it, but she really played it up, acting embarrassed and trying to get out of it before finally stripping off and spreading herself out in a chair. She took ages, pretending she found it hard to get off with everyone watching, but really enjoying herself, teasing her tits and pussy, stroking her belly the way she liked to, putting her fingers in and licking them, all the while getting gradually more and more turned on, until at last she lost control completely and rolled herself up in the chair, her arsehole on show as well as her pussy and she rubbed herself to a really noisy orgasm. I took her upstairs to the straight after and fucked her over Neil's bed.

The second time was maybe even better, because it wasn't sorted out in advance and I wasn't going out with the girl who did it, even though without me there it would never have happened. She was called Ella, and she was a real firebrand, you know, one of these girls who's dead sure men think women always need to be led and will do anything to prove otherwise. We'd been drinking a good bit at a party in Fulham, and the conversation had got around to how women are more precious about their bodies, or that was what two of the guys there were saying anyway. Ella wasn't having it, and I saw my chance. I told her to put her money where her mouth was and strip off. She came right back, telling me she would if I would. I stripped off, and after a bit of backchat and trying to get out of it, so did she, because there was no way she was going to back down. I didn't really think it would go any further, but I had to give it a try and started saying all she'd showed was that she could follow a man's lead. She was not happy about that, but when I suggested she prove it by frigging off in front of everybody you should've seen her eyes pop. I played it cool, saying I'd do it if she didn't have the guts, and when she told me to stop being a filthy bastard I just gave this little shrug, like I'd proved my point and wasn't interested any more. That stung her, and it took me another half an hour but I got her in the end, flat on her back in front of the fireplace, playing with her pussy and tits until she made it, and boy did she scream. And another thing, when her knickers came down she was absolutely soaking, so I reckon she'd been horny more or less from the start.

Both those times were really good, but the girls were getting themselves off, so it wasn't really like they couldn't help it. There's another trick of mine, maybe not quite so dirty, but good. I used to do it with Sammy. When your car needs petrol, find some excuse to get her to use the pump, then come up behind her and take over, with your arms around her so she can't get away, your hands on the lever and the hose between her legs. She'll probably struggle a bit once she realises what you're doing, but once you get the pump going she's not going to fight that hard. The vibrations are something else, and if you've gut the hose pushed right up tight against her pussy it's like she's got a giant-sized vibrator between her legs. Once I'd got Sammy used to it she couldn't get enough. Every time we needed to fill up she'd be straight out of the car and she'd take the pump in this provocative way, with her bum just stuck out a little, like she was posing. I'd get a grip on her and push the hose tight in between her legs, then turn the flow on. Sometimes she'd make it, sometimes she wouldn't, but at the very least it would leave her badly in need of sex, so badly I'd generally have to take advantage of the state she was in before we got home, parked up somewhere quiet, or once or twice in a dogging car park so she'd know she was being watched while she got her fucking doggy style with the seats laid back. I tried the same with a few other girls as well, and like with Sammy sometimes they made it, sometimes not, but it always turned them on. That's the only drawback with petrol pumps. You have to stop once the tank is full, but the state it leaves the girls in I'm not sure it's such a drawback after all.

It was after I split up with Sammy that I started to get into bondage. This girl called Naomi, who I met at the gym, introduced me to it one night, because she wanted her wrists tied to her bedposts while I fucked her. I was only too happy to oblige, and too pissed and horny to do any more than give her a good seeing to, but what she'd asked for gave me an idea. The next time we met I told her I'd tie her up and she willingly agreed, only this time I did it properly, with her wrists and ankles tied securely to the bed posts and her spread-eagled naked on the bed, only instead of giving her a good hard fucking, which was what she was into, I frigged her off, taking my time until I'd made her come, and only then climbing on top. She howled the house down at first, so loud I had to stuff her knickers in her mouth and tie them off with a spare piece of rope to shut her up, but afterwards she admitted she'd loved it and for the rest of the time we were together she couldn't get enough.

The problem was she was married, to a boring arse of a solicitor who thought she needed to see a shrink to get rid of her love of being tied up. She'd been, the shrink had listened to her for three sessions at a couple of hundred quid a shot, then on the third he'd tied her hands behind her back with her tights, spanked her bottom and fucked her on his couch. He didn't charge for that session, and after that she told her husband she was cured and got her kicks elsewhere. That just goes to show, if you wife's kinky, make the best of it and don't moan.

One of the guys she went with was some sort of bondage guru she'd met on the net. He could tie her up so tight she couldn't do more than wiggle her toes, or put knots in places so that every little movement was like being given an erotic massage, only all over at the same time. She learnt a few of the techniques and passed them on to me, and if I could never get the hang of the fancy stuff, by the end any girl I tied up wasn't going anywhere, and she probably was going to come.

My favourite was a sort of harness, tied so that it enclosed the girl's body but didn't restrict her arms, with flat plaques of rope over her nipples and a big knot right in the middle of her pussy so that it would rub on her clit as she walked. The idea was it could be worn all day, but it showed through unless she was wearing a winter coat, which was how I used it on my next girlfriend, Sophie. Sophie was a little curvy thing, all bum and tit, great for getting off over and ever so willing to please. She had a bit of a hang-up about her weight, although I thought she was sex on a stick, and used to try and compensate by being a dirty bitch. That was something I was not about to put a stop to, especially when it came to being my plaything for kinky experiments to make her come.

I put her in the harness one day in the winter and took her out walking, through the local park where there were lots of people about. With Naomi she used to take ten, maybe fifteen minutes before she'd come, but either I hadn't tied it quiet right or Sophie was less sensitive, because she took ages. It turned her on all right, until she was wriggling in her panties and begging me to take her back to the flat for a good fucking. I wouldn't do it, because I loved to see her squirm, so I made her keep walking, all the while getting more and more turned on, until she couldn't stop herself from wriggling her hips to try and make it happen. When it hit her she went down on her knees, gasping and sobbing and calling me a pig, but later she admitted it was the best orgasm she'd ever had. It was good for me too, not just from the way she reacted, but because at least five people were watching when she came, and afterwards, with her kneeling on the bed and her hands tied behind her back while she sucked me off with her bum bare and a vibrator stuck up her hole, that's what I came over.

I had a great time with Sophie. She wasn't quite like Sammy, who got off on being given orders, but she was always willing to try and once she was turned on there was no stopping her. She used to like toys as well, and we'd go into the sex shops in the city centre to look for new stuff. Some of it cost a bit, and one time I asked the guy behind the counter if he'd give us fifty per cent off if she did her business in front of him. I hadn't asked her, and she went bright red, but she did it, with her skirt up and a vibrator pushed down the front of her knickers while she brought herself off and he watched. That was great, even better than when he offered to let us have our stuff for free if I'd make her give him a blow job in the back. She didn't need telling, because that was just the sort of dirty stuff that got her off, as long as she was the centre of attention and felt desirable. Apparently he came all over her tits and said they were the best he'd ever had, which she seemed to like.

One toy we got was a remote-controlled vibrator. I suppose it worked something like a car alarm or a walkie talkie, because up to about half a mile I could use the remote control to turn it on or off, which controlled a vibrating love egg she would wear down her knickers. She loved it when we used it close to home, and it did make me feel good, just to have that much control over her. The only problem was that I had to be close to see her come and she preferred not to know when it was going to happen, so while it was good it wasn't the best. I went a bit far in the end. She had a job in the city, and used to sit in on important meetings, I made her wear the egg one day and told her I'd switch it on when the train started to get near our local station, so she would come with all the commuters around her. Instead I went in myself, stood underneath the windows of her office and then turned it on. She wasn't best pleased about that, and while there was a lot of other shit going on I think that was what put our relationship on the slide.

I had a bit of a gap after Sophie, one or two one-night stands and one or two girls I'd tie up so they could get their rocks off, but nothing serious. What I did do was improve my bondage skills, until I could not only tie a girl so she was completely helpless but do it fast and, if I had to, undo her just as fast. That's useful, because it means you can take risks you wouldn't be able to otherwise, or at least it is if you've got the right girl.

Leonie was the right girl. I met her at one of the bondage classes, where she was saying it was all too detached for her taste and she wanted something more down to earth. Down to earth I could give her, and that evening I tied her up on my bed and used a vibrator on her until she'd come three times and was so high on sex she let me put it up her bum. I'd never done that before, and it felt good, especially when I used the vibrator on her a fourth time and she came with my cock in her hole. That felt like I was being milked up her arse, and by the time she finished I had been.

It was all a bit different with Leonie. She knew as much as I did, maybe more, and she knew a lot of friends who were into the same sort of stuff. It was great to meet people who understood me, because I'd always felt a bit of a lone pervert, for all that most of the girls I'd been with loved what I did. With Leonie and her friends it was different, really easygoing, and we even had a few foursomes, with other couples and sharing the girls. That was great, especially the night we tied Leonie and a girl called Claire head to tail and made them lick each other out before we'd let them go. Not that they needed much encouragement.

It was Claire's boyfriend, Dave, who taught me a new trick, how to spank a girl to orgasm. More than one of my exes had liked her bum slapped, but I'd never really been into the whole spanking thing. Dave showed me that nearly as much went into it as bondage, and one night, to prove his point, he spanked Claire in front of us until she came. Now that was worth seeing. She was a pretty little thing, with not much tit to speak of but a lovely round bum, nice and cheeky. He did it with her over his knee, her skirt lifted up and her knickers pulled down, which was how he liked her, and spent the best part of an hour slowly warming her up until her bum was pink all over. She was already moaning when he started to smack over her pussy, using firm, even slaps that got gradually faster. Her moans rose in time to the spanking, getting louder and more excited, until she finally went into orgasm, and for all my experience I don't think I've ever seen a girl so powerless to stop what was happening to her.

I had to try it with Leonie, only I wanted to do it with her tied up and gagged as well. It took a bit of practice, and I had to do it in my own style, but eventually I worked it out. I had her tied in a great position, kneeling down over a stool with her thighs tied to the legs so that she couldn't close them, her hands behind her back and her body lashed to the top of the stool. That left her bum stuck right up, and wide open, with everything showing and available to me, while she was at just the right height to put my cock in her mouth or her pussy, even up her bum, whatever I wanted, but first I was going to beat her to orgasm.

Dave had spanked Claire, but I found I got better control using a riding whip with a particularly broad end, just the right size to smack the sensitive area around Leonie's pussy and arsehole. It stung a lot more too, or so she said, which made it easier to get her bum nice and hot before getting down to the real business. She was great, squirming and gasping through her gag as I whipped her, crying out and shaking her head for the pain, but never once asking me to stop, and getting more and more turned on. It took me about half an hour to make her come, and when she did the contractions of her body were so hard she nearly had the stool over. That had me going with a vengeance and I took full advantage of her, first in her mouth once I'd pulled the gag out, then up her pussy and finishing off all over her well whipped bum.

It was a great technique, even if you could only do it once a week or so, and of course it's far too kinky to be done in public or anything like. We did do it at a party, in front of Dave and Claire and two other couples, but it was that sort of party, which is a different sort of thrill. She was also keen on something a bit more public, although what really got her off was the idea of other people seeing her get a spanking and thinking it was for real. I liked the idea, especially if whoever saw it thought she was getting a real punishment, she got so turned on she couldn't help coming.

I had to pay for it in the end, sort of, but it was worth it, because I did her in a way that had her shaking with excitement just the first time I explained what I was going to do. Two months and a lot of organising later we were in Amsterdam, at a brothel that specialises in floor shows. I'd fixed it so that their regulars would get an offer of the chance to watch one of the girls punished, which meant that the punters thought Leonie was getting it for real and she loved that. I did her on stage, with her tied down over a whipping stool by me and

40

two big Dutch guys, just the way she'd been before, knees apart and bum stuck up in the air, only this time with a couple of dozen horny sex tourists to watch. They were real bastards, all of them getting off on seeing her led out and bent over and tied up in that position. Some of them even had their cocks out before I'd got her knickers pulled down, and not one of them objected, for all that she was pretending to fight and kept begging us to stop, at least she did until I'd gagged her. They loved her beating too, and half of them had come long before she did, but when she did it was like an explosion, and they really loved that, seeing a girl punished, badly, but so turned on by what was being done to her that she climaxed under the whip. I'm still with Leonie, and we've got another booking in a couple of months, so if you happen to be in Amsterdam …

STUART — Fulham

Miss Prissy

Leila Hunt was a teacher at the local secondary school. We saw her go past our office every morning and back in the afternoon, so perfect with her smart heel clip-clopping up the road, her slim legs in stockings, her knee-length skirt and jacket, her crisp white blouse and the little black ribbon tie she always wore. It was like a uniform for her and any other woman would have looked frumpy in it. Not Leila, because even with her glasses and her hair up in a tight bun she was a dream. Just to watch her bum wiggle under that skirt made my cock stand to attention, and for all her effort to look neat and respectable it was obvious she had a hard job finding blouses that would hold her in properly without being too baggy around her waist. Stripped down she'd have looked like a centrefold.

I wanted her from the first day I saw her,

and I thought, why not? She was in her late twenties, not much younger than me, and if I wasn't quite in her league looks-wise, then I'm not a bad catch. My income running my own letting agency had to be three times what hers was for a start, so you'd think she would at least have been up for a date to see how we got on. Not a bit of it. I thought I played it well, looking sharp when I approached her, making sure she saw the 7 series and knew it was mine, asking a straight question: could I buy her a coffee or a glass of wine at the place across the road?

I didn't just get turned down. I got looked at as if I was a flasher, or some dirty old man who'd asked if she'd give him the knickers she was wearing, seriously. Her nose went up in the air, she gave a little sniff and walked straight on by, still wiggling that sexy little rump all the way to the corner. I'd expected at least a smile, and I was so taken aback I just stood there in the street, gaping like a goldfish. The boys in the office thought it was hilarious, but I noticed that none of them tried their luck, because every single one of them knew that if that was the reaction I got then he'd get worse.

We reckoned she had to be a lesbian. It was the only explanation that made sense. After all, if she was with somebody she'd still have been flattered and could either have given me a polite refusal or taken a chance that I might prove a better deal than the boyfriend. If she had no interest at all, then it had to be that she preferred girls. That was a thought to make you sweat. I mean, what a waste, to think of that gorgeous woman out of bounds because she's a carpet muncher, but that wasn't so bad, because at least if I wasn't going to get to dip my wick, then nor was anybody else. No, what really got me was the thought of her getting down to it with her girlfriend. I couldn't see her with some hairy diesel dyke, she just had too much class. Whoever she was with would be just as good-looking, slim and smart and sexy, maybe another teacher, or some sort of professional anyway.

I could imagine it, all too easily, the two of them laughing together over the way she'd turned me down. The girlfriend kissing her, right on the lips. Fingers going to blouse buttons, undoing them, opening the sides over those magnificent tits, her bra undone and slipped off down her sleeve the way girls do, then all that flesh bare, round and bouncy and naked in her girlfriend's hands, to be felt and kissed and sucked until they're both so turned on they do it in the hall, maybe a sixty-nine with their smart suits dishevelled and their pussies in each other's face. Like I said, it's enough to make you sweat.

We never did see her with another girl, and one of the boys, I forget who, suggested she might like geeks instead. Well, intellectuals, if you prefer, one of her fellow teachers perhaps, some egghead in a scruffy suit and his hair all over the place, probably with a five-year-old Volvo and a house full of pretentious books. That was worse, if anything, to think of a man like that with her, touching that beautiful body, his clumsy hands undressing her, feeling up her tits and bum, and her putting up with it because she thinks he's clever and never knowing what she's missing. Bu then, we never saw her with a bloke like that either, or anybody else.

It was just the same every morning and every afternoon, clip-clop one way along the road and clip-clop back the other. I thought about having another go, reckoning that maybe she'd been on her monthly or something, but the way she'd reacted before put me off and I did not want the boys to see me get the brush-off a second time. So I contented myself with watching, and with undressing her in my mind, but I hadn't given up. All the while I was wondering what the secret was, because if there's one thing I've learnt down the years it's that there's always a way into a woman's knickers. You just have to find it.

Okay, for some guys it's hopeless. If you look like a complete fucking pig and you're broke and you smell, you're getting nowhere. Then some girls are really into older guys, and of course there's lesbians. So maybe one woman in twenty isn't up for it no matter what unless you're a sugar daddy, or another girl, or whatever. The rest are game, and it doesn't matter a toss if they're married, or going out with somebody or what. I know they always go on about love and being faithful, but it's all bullshit. Get them horny and set it up so they reckon they're safe, and you are in, my son.

The boys had nicknamed Leila "Miss Prissy" and reckoned she was unobtainable, but I couldn't help thinking of her as Leila, or even Miss Hunt, which seemed to suit her, and I hadn't given up. I thought maybe she just needed a bit of time to get over herself, and so I tried the friendly approach, giving her a little smile when we happened to pass in the street, and making sure we did quite a lot. She ignored me like I didn't exist.

I was sure she'd noticed me, because she had to have done, and reckoned that maybe she was one of those girls who like a man to make a lot of effort before she'll even look at them. I did my best, carefully avoiding the office and the boys so they wouldn't take the piss, first off asking her for directions so she at least had to speak to me, even though from the look on her face she knew full well I was trying one on. Next I tried the old spare ticket routine, with seats for some poncy Shakespeare play, which is what I reckoned she'd be into. All I got was a cold "No thank you". When I got down on one knee right in front of her with a huge bunch of flowers and a bottle of champagne she couldn't ignore me, or so I thought. She crossed the road.

After that I gave up, mainly because I

didn't want her thinking I was some kind of stalker. Anyway, I was knocking up this nice little Turkish piece from one of the local restaurants, very smart, with an arse like a watermelon and tits you could drown in. Unfortunately she was the marrying kind, and I didn't like the way her dad used to strop his kebab knife when I came to call for her, so I had to drop it. That was a pain, but seeing Miss Prissy clip-clop past that same afternoon reminded me what I really wanted, and what I wasn't going to get.

I did my best to put it all out of my mind, because that kind of stuff fucks up work and when it comes down to it I know the bottom line: money. We'd got some new property on the books, a big old house that had been full of squatters but only needed a bit of elbow grease and a lick of paint to make a nice set of one-bedroom flats. That's what Mark reckoned anyway, so I put it on the boards and went down to have a look.

It was more like the place had been full of pigs, and we had the council coming round on the Monday, so it looked like I was going to have to get my hands dirty and it was going to be a working weekend. That's the trouble with being the boss. I got down to it on the Sunday, sweeping and shovelling and scrubbing and Christ knows what, just to make it look as if it hadn't been condemned. All morning that took me, and most of the afternoon, until I looked like I was on the bins. Which is when Miss Prissy walks in.

Of all the luck. I mean, I'm a smart guy. I never let it slip, even when I'm at home, except very rarely when work means I have to. If my chances had been slim before, now I was stuffed, but she was looking for a flat and that stupid bastard Mark had given her the keys on the Saturday without telling me. I had to show her around: what else could I do?

Just the way she was wrinkling that perfect little nose made me feel like a tramp, only she didn't seem to be in a hurry at all. She wanted to look around all six of the bedsits, in every room, and when she'd been right round she asked to see the garden as well. I tried to put her off, because it looked liked a rubbish tip, but she wasn't having it. There was even this shed at the back, so full of shit that you wouldn't believe it. You could hardly get in the door, but she has to have a look. So in she goes and I'm standing outside when she calls to me. I went in, thinking she was going to give me a bollocking for showing her a place in such a state, but she's standing there, or not exactly standing, more propped up against a pile of old linoleum rolls, looking thoughtful and licking her lips. Now I know a randy girl when I see one, but I couldn't figure this out at all. There she is, as smart at ever, those big old tits looking like they're going to burst out of her blouse, with her nips poking up through the silk, looking like she's ready for bed, only in this dirty old shed with me looking like a tramp or something. I didn't know what to say, but she did. She says, "It's Stuart, isn't it? You like me, don't you? Why don't you show me?" This and she's looking right at my crotch, then again, "Go on, show me, take it out."

No woman needs to say that to me twice, especially not a doll like her, and if she wanted to play funny games, well, I wasn't going to stop her. So I unzipped my overalls and pulled it all out, showing her what I'd got, and she's staring and licking her lips. "That's nice," she says, "get it hard for me." I'd got over my

53

surprise by then, so I told her that was her job, and do you know what she says? "Make me do it then."

So I did. I got her by the hair and pulled her down on the floor, kneeling on the dirty concrete. I stuck my cock in her mouth and she got sucking like she'd never had it so good. By then I'd got her figured. She liked it dirty, just the opposite to the way she normally was, and the state she'd got me in I was ready to give it to her. There was more than that and all. After the way she'd treated me, all those snotty little glances and walking past with her nose in the air, I tell you I was getting a real kick out of it as I started to get hard in her mouth. Her hair was in a bun, like always, only my hands were locked in it real tight and it was starting to come to bits. If that turned her on, getting down and dirty in that filthy shack, that was just fine by me, and I had to say I liked it too. She was so perfect, and so stuck-up, to have my cock stuck in her mouth with her kneeling on the filthy floor was great, but I wasn't going to settle for just a blow job. I ordered her to get her tits out.

She didn't even hesitate, still sucking away

as her fingers went to her blouse, and she couldn't get those buttons undone fast enough. I'd imagined that so many times, and now it was real, her blouse coming apart to show off those big, round tits, all soft and white and lovely, each one cupped in cream coloured lace. I told her to pull the bra up and flop them out, and out they came, bigger even than I'd imagined, and now she was showing them off her sucking had got even more eager. I reckoned maybe it was the way I was talking to her, partly, so I tried a bit more, telling her to feel her tits and that I was going to fuck them. She liked that, giving me a last kiss on my knob and kneeling up to wrap them around my hard cock. I told her what I was doing, titty fucking her, and what I might do, give her a facial, only at that she says, really breathless, "You've got to fuck me first."

I told her I'd fuck her. I told her I'd fuck her up the arse, just to be dirty, but at that she gave a moan and the next moment she's jumped up, to bend over this old table with her tits swinging in all these cobwebs and crap and her little arse stuck up ready. I came up behind her and jerked her jacket and blouse down behind her back so her arms are trapped and she's got no choice but to lie there with her tits on the filthy table top, her face too. I took her by the hair and pulled it out, which made her gasp and start begging me to do it. I was going to, but I was in no hurry, not with all that on offer.

She looked great from behind, with those smart little clip-clop shoes and her stockings going up under her skirt, with her neat little bum all round and inviting underneath but her top half a mess with her jacket and blouse down, her bra pulled up and those big tits filthy and heaving. I pulled up her skirt, really slowly, to see her stocking tops and the slices of creamy white thighs above, then her knickers, fancy French ones to match her bra, all tight over the sweetest little bum you ever did see, firm and high and cheeky, with her slit showing through the lacy panel in the back. She told me to pull them down, in this really dirty voice, and I did it, nice and slow, easing them off her bum to bare her, those perfect little cheeks and everything else. She was shaved, her arsehole a tight pink star with smooth skin all around, her cunt a perfect little split fig, all wet and ready in the middle. I put a finger up, and that made her moan again, so I followed up with my cock. She was tight, not a virgin, but tight, so for all that she was creamy it took a couple of good shoves before I could get it right in. She was loving it, moaning and gasping as I humped her, so I took a tit in each hand and laid in, giving it to her as fast as I could.

I was enjoying the view, like any man would, but it was more than that. This was Miss Prissy, the stuck-up bitch who hadn't even bothered to acknowledge me, for all the effort I'd made, and here she was, bent over a table in some filthy shack with her tits out and my cock up her from behind, with that perfect little bum jiggling as I stuck myself in and out. I started to play with her, taking my cock out and sticking it back in just to watch the way her cunt opened to my knob. I was telling her that too, those words, and she loved it, but best of all, she liked it when I told her she had a pretty arsehole and I had a good mind to put my cock up it. She was game, and even though I'd never given a woman a bum shag in my life, now was the time.

I went down, licking her arse, which had her gasping like she was going to come. She opened up nicely too, so I could soon put a finger up, then two. That looked even better, with her bum framed in the mess of her clothes, skirt pulled up and knickers down, her cheeks open and two fingers in her arsehole, her cunt open and dripping juicy down her legs, just so fucking filthy, and I'd thought she was such a prissy little bitch.

She was begging for it, and she got it, my cock stuck slowly up her arse, bit by bit, her hole pushing in until her ring spread and then all tight and pink and glistening where her anus was stretched tight around my shaft. I put it right up, until my balls were squashed to her cunt, a good, deep buggering, which was exactly what she wanted. When I started to row her I did it slow, and bent back, so I could watch her arsehole pull in and out on my cock, just to get the sight of her with her ring fucked right into my head. She was loving it, gasping and moaning and begging me to go faster, and she'd even reached back for her cunt, to frig herself, just the filthiest thing I'd ever seen, a girl rubbing her cunt to get off while there's a cock up her arse.

Christ but it felt good when she came. Her ring went tight on my cock, just like a cunt, and I nearly gave her my load up her arse. I'd have done it too, only suddenly she's begging for something more, something so fucking filthy I wasn't sure I'd heard her right the first time. "Now in my mouth," she says. "Put it in my mouth."

Twice more she said it, and even then I hesitated. I mean, I'd got it up her bumhole, and she wanted to suck me! Only then I remember how she'd treated me. So out comes my cock, leaving her arsehole looking like you could drive a freight train up it, and in her mouth it goes. And she's sucking, still rubbing her cunt and sucking my dirty cock, and I have never, ever seen so much pleasure on a woman's face. She came a second time, and so did I, right down her throat while she's sucking me like she's trying to swallow me whole. Some of it came out, all around her lips and over my balls, so I whipped out my cock and rubbed it in her face, smearing spunk all over those pretty, prissy features, all over her glasses and in her hair, then stuck it back in her mouth and held her nose to make her swallow.

And that was that, Miss Prissy, only maybe not quite so prissy after all.

ED — Paris

Too Good to be True

Lucie was one of the prettiest and sexiest girls I'd ever been out with, but after just a few days I knew it wasn't going to work. I like a girl to be mine, if you know what I mean. I'm not some kind of jealousy freak who goes after ex boyfriends or anything, but when I'm with a girl I don't look at other girls or flirt and I expect the same in return. Lucie could never be like that. Maybe she was just too lovely, and too wild. She had the classic French look, very petite, with dark hair and a face full of mischief, with great big, dark eyes, a mouth like a rosebud and a tiny nose with freckles either side, perky tits and a pert bum. Not surprisingly a lot of men fancied her, but she seemed to know everybody, so that we'd be walking down the street or having a coffee on the pavement when some random bloke would stop to talk to her, kiss her, maybe hug her, all of which she'd return with the same warmth. Not that she was bad to me, because a lot of them would try to cut me out but she'd always do the introductions and always say I was her boyfriend. She liked to go to these clubs too, really wild places where it was even worse. There were even some guys who seemed to think it was okay to greet her with a slap on the bum, and it was after I threatened to hit one of them that we had our first row. She just couldn't see it. As far as she was concerned I was the one she went to bed with at the end of the day and that should have been enough. I wasn't having it and laid down the law. She agreed, but I still didn't feel comfortable, and when I met Heather I told Lucie we were finished.

Heather was everything Lucie wasn't, English for a start, in Paris for work, like me. I work for an investment bank and although I work hard, I have plenty of time, and money, to enjoy myself. She was tall and blonde and quite busty, which I like and I'd never really been satisfied with Lucie's tiny pair, however firm and perky. Unfortunately it didn't last with Heather either. She was ready for commitment, a family, the works, and I wasn't. So that was that, no girlfriend, and to be really honest I felt I could do with a break, although I knew I'd be after the first cutie who gave me the eye.

And they did. I'd been in Paris over a year, and I knew the girls were a bit less precious than in England, but I was not expecting a completely gorgeous brunette to sit down at my table at my favourite place in the Avenue de Suffren and ask if she could buy me a drink. Not me buy her a drink, but the other way around! It's quite close to the Eiffel Tower, and my first thought was that she was a pro and I'd misheard what she'd said. I was going to give her a polite refusal, but the waiter was right by our table and before I could say anything she'd ordered a white wine for herself and another beer for me. I thought she was trying to take me for a ride and it must have shown in my face, because she quickly reassured me and then told me she knew Lucie.

I wasn't quite sure how things stood with Lucie, because I'd finished it by email and she hadn't replied, but the girl seemed friendly and she was gorgeous. I was still a bit cautious, but it was hard to keep it up with her chatting away in this soft, husky voice that seemed to go straight to my cock. She was called Mirella and she was a Brazilian student studying languages. I thought that might explain things, if she was broke and knew there was a single guy on a good salary to be had. That was just fine by me, and she was flirting so openly it was obvious what she wanted.

I took it easy, insisting on paying for the drinks when the bill arrived and asking if she'd like to come back to my apartment, with the obvious implication that it would be for a bit of afternoon delight. She accepted, and the rest of the afternoon was like something out of a wet dream. She was a big girl, maybe an inch shorter than I am, and while I reckoned her chest had had a bit of silicone assistance it was certainly impressive. She was completely cool about it too.

You know how most girls like to pretend it's all chocolates and flowers even when they're getting really dirty? Mirella wasn't like that. She knew what men like and was only too happy to provide, at least for as much as she wanted to give. We'd barely got through the door before she'd slipped the top of her dress down, asking quite frankly what I thought. I thought plenty, and I told her so. She had quite dark skin, mixed maybe, like a lot of Brazilians, and very smooth and soft, with a lovely smell, like cocoa butter or something. Each tit was a heavy, round ball, very firm, and topped by a dark, stiff nipple.

She said I could touch and I took one in each hand, feeling how big they were and rubbing my thumbs over her nipples to get her horny. At that she pulled my head in, between them first, then putting my mouth to each of her nipples in turn. By then I was rock hard, but when I tried to pull her dress further down she stopped me and told me, straight out, that I couldn't fuck her but she was going to give me the best blow job I'd ever had. A lot of girls don't like to put it all out on the first date, so for all that she'd been so horny with me I didn't complain.

It was the best blow job of my life and all.

She did me in an armchair, down on her knees between my legs with her lovely big tits out. A lot of girls don't like to kneel to man, but there was no bullshit with Mirella. She really worked on it, and she obviously didn't just like cock, she loved it. Just from the look in her eyes as she unzipped me I could tell it was as big a treat for her as it was for me, and she didn't hold back at all. She took out my balls as well as my cock, kissed them and took them in her mouth, one by one, which was almost too much. Once she'd got my cock in her mouth she was still playing with my balls, and gently tugging on my shaft.

She used her tits too, wrapping them around my cock and jiggling them about as well as letting me titty fuck her and licking my knob, rubbing her nipples on my balls and shaft too. She really knew what she was doing, doing stuff like kissing my knob and suddenly sucking it into her mouth, and running her tongue up and down the extra sensitive bit on the underside of my foreskin.

It took all my willpower not to spunk over her inside the first minute, but I was determined to make it last. So was she, pacing herself and teasing by doing something to take me to the edge and then pulling back to give me a show of her boobs, but always coming back to my cock. I'd heard the term cock worship before, but while I'd known plenty of girls who liked to suck this was the real thing, as if she was in love with my cock and couldn't get enough. She even asked me if I'd like to spunk in her mouth or over her face and tits, and no girl has ever done that for me before.

I chose her face and tits, because I wanted to see how she'd look with that pretty, bold face and those huge titties all spattered with spunk. She went for it, coming up close and grinning and laughing as she took turns to toss my cock and rub it over her tits. I couldn't hold, not for long, not with her gripping my cock like that and tugging up and down while she rubbed my knob over her nipples. I did it, all over her tits and in her face, with her holding me and wanking like crazy, and deliberately aiming so my spurts would go all over her, and if I'd never known a girl who loved cock so much then I'd never known a girl so loved spunk so much either.

She really got off on making a mess of herself, using my cock to rub what I'd done over her face and tits, even licking bits off her nipples and using her fingers to scoop it up, then sucking them clean and all the while with her eyes looking right into mine. She sucked my cock clean too, and swallowed like a good girl should. Even though I'd just come I really enjoyed the show, and would have got hard for her again as soon as I could if she'd wanted me to.

She didn't, but before she left she told me three things, that she was a virgin and her pussy was out of bounds, that she didn't want a relationship but would like to meet again, and that I had a lovely cock. All that was fine by me. As she was Brazilian she was presumably a Catholic and wanted to get married still a virgin, although the way she sucked cock her future husband was never going to believe she was innocent. I didn't want a relationship either, but I wasn't about to turn down the prospect of regular, no-strings blowjobs, and I'd already figured out that she thought I had a lovely cock.

The next day I could scarcely believe it had happened, but it had, and just the memory of that blowjob kept me going all week. I even saw Lucie, and if she was a bit distant she didn't have a go at me or anything, so I

70

mentioned that I'd met a friend of hers and got a smile back, like she was happy for me. That surprised me, but you never can tell with women and I decided that perhaps she'd been keen to end it and was pleased things had gone the way they had.

I was hoping to see Mirella at the weekend, but when I phoned her number all I could get was her voicemail. She had mentioned something about going away, although not immediately, so I wasn't all that surprised. I did go to my usual place on the Saturday lunchtime, hoping she might come past and getting fairly horny just watching the girls go by. One was particularly fine, a sassy little black girl, very slim, with a little round bum perched on the longest legs I'd ever seen and barely covered by her little black dress, which was tight on her waist and chest but loose at her thighs so that you thought all it needed was the tiniest puff of wind and she'd be showing her knickers, if she had any on.

I watched her walk one way, and she seemed to be looking for a house, which gave me plenty of opportunity to admire her legs. Once she'd gone a little way she turned back, still looking, and then came into the cafe, spoke to the barman and came over to my table, smiling and asking if I was indeed Edward. I told her she'd got it right and offered to buy her a drink. She was called Samara and she was Mirella's flat-mate. Mirella was out of town, but had sent her with a message, apologising for not being there for me and asking if Samara would do instead.

She said all this quite casually, and when she'd finished there was a wicked little smile on her face. I was astonished, but if that was their idea of good manners I wasn't going to turn her down, not in a hurry. Then she leans forward and whispers into my ear, telling her friend had said I had a lovely cock and that she'd like to suck it.

I nearly came in my pants. Five minutes I'd known her and she was offering to suck me off, and there was more too. When we'd got back to my apartment she told me she was going to strip for me. She sat me down in the same armchair as before, kissing me as she unzipped my trousers and pulled out my cock and balls, every bit at ease as Mirella but if anything even more skilled. She was more patient anyway, giving me a little suck just to get me going and then walking over to the kitchen with her cute little bum wiggling behind her. She fetched me a cold beer, took a swallow and then went down on me again, only with her mouth full of ice-cold Chimay. I took the bottle as she sucked, and I swear I was crossed-eyed with pleasure.

She soon got up, filled the glass she'd been holding with beer and stepped back into the middle of the room. She didn't bother with music, and she'd not dance so much as flaunt herself, but she was good. Like Mirella, she knew how to please a man, with no arty-farty stuff and lots of bum and tit. She was a tease too, taking for ever before her dress came down off her shoulders and keeping her tits covered with her hands even when it had. She was nice up top as well, not as big as Mirella, but firm and shapely, each one a good handful of firm black flesh topped by tiny nipples that were even darker. She had a lovely bum too, and she really made the best of it, first flirting with her dress to make it come up and show off the little white panties and slices of firm black bum cheeks beneath, then slowly wriggling it down over her hips, a bit at a time, only to stop, and a bit more, until at last she pulled it up instead and tucked it up into its own waistband. Her bum looked better still in just panties, small and tight and round, good enough to lick, and when she began to ease those little white panties down the same way she had her dress I was sure I was going to pop.

She must have realised, because she tucked the panties down under her cheeks to give me a last show of her sexy little bum and then came swaying over to get down on her knees and take me back in her mouth. Her skill was the deep throat, taking my cock right in deep until you wouldn't have thought she could breathe, and when she came up again telling me I could fuck her mouth and not to worry about making her gag. That's another offer you don't get from girls very often, and I made the best of it, taking her by the hair and giving that pretty black face a good hard fucking, my cock pumping in and out between those luscious, painted lips until at last I couldn't take it any more and spunked up down her throat. Like Mirella, she swallowed, and like Mirella she was well pleased with herself and content with having pleasured me. I offered her a lick in return, mainly because I was keen to get to grips with that tight black bum, maybe even tongue her bumhole, but she said no, giving me the same reason as her friend had. She also told me I had a lovely cock and said she'd be back.

So that was how it stood, two gorgeous Brazilian girls, not girlfriends and not wanting to be, but regular suck buddies. They made it plain that I had to respect their boundaries, but that wasn't a problem, especially after the third incident. I suppose every man likes the idea of having two girls at the same time, especially if they're into each other, but not many get it. I hadn't, not then, so when Mirella and Samara turned up at my flat together the following weekend I thought the best I could hope for was for one of them to take me into my bedroom for my blowjob while the other stayed outside.

There was none of that. I'd barely sat them down with a drink each and Samara says she wants to see my cock again, with Mirella nodding agreement and saying how big I am and how much she enjoyed sucking me, and this in front of each other. You don't get that in England, or in France. At least, I hadn't, but these two were up for it, more than just up for it, eager for it.

Anything to please a lady, so I unzipped and pulled out my cock and balls, the way they seemed to like it, asking for them to get their tits out in return. They both responded without a second thought, Mirella pushing down the tight red dress she was wearing and pulling off the lacy black bra underneath, and Samara peeling up her red and white striped top to show them bare. Both their nipples were already perky, and my cock was getting that way too. They asked me to let them watch me get hard and I obliged, slowly teasing myself erect, and before I was halfway there they'd began to play with each others' tits. It was for real too. They were getting off on each other, but that didn't stop them putting on a show at the same time, making sure I could see as they felt each other, kissing as they touched each others tits, then taking turns to suck on the hard, dark nipples.

Soon I was rock hard, and they started to

get really horny with each other, in a tangle on the sofa with their hands all over each others bodies, bums as well as tits and their mouths locked together. I was going to spunk, and I'd have been content with that, but Mirella suddenly pulled back and gave Samara a playful little slap on the hand, telling her friend that they were neglecting me. I told them I didn't mind, but Samara answered straight out that she didn't want to miss out on my cock and that Mirella was right.

They crawled over to me, tits swinging under their chests and bums stuck up, and if what they'd done before had been good, this was wild. It was like they were desperate too. They pulled down my trousers first, then both of them set to work. They just could not get enough of my cock, taking turns to suck and lick while the other dealt with my balls or wanked me into her friend's mouth, Samara even licking my arse while Mirella sucked me, and all the time sharing cock-flavoured kisses and touching up each others' tits.

Like before, it took all my willpower to hold back, and as it was I didn't last all that long. With Samara's tongue in my arsehole and my cock in Mirella's mouth while they showed off playing with each others' tits it was more than I could stand. I came in Mirella's mouth, only for her to jerk back after the first spurt and deliberately take the rest in her face, and there was plenty. She kept her mouth open, but it didn't all go in, one long streamer landing across her eye and down her cheek, then another catching her on the nose, so that as she finally pulled back she was left with a pool of white stuff on her tongue, her face streaked with it and a blob hanging from her nose.

I was spent, but they weren't. Samara came up from licking my arse and to my amazement they began to share my spunk, first Samara licking it up off Mirella's face and then both of them sharing their mouthful with their lips just touching as they rolled what they had in their mouths back and forth. I have never, ever seen anything so horny, not outside of a hardcore porno movie.

That was what got me thinking, that maybe the two of them were pros after all, only not streetwalkers but porn stars. It still seemed odd that they'd be so into me, but it did explain their behaviour. Not that I cared, because good sex is good sex and they'd both made it perfectly clear that our relationship would be casual. I didn't actually want to get with either of them on a permanent basis either although I couldn't quite figure out why. The sex was great, don't get me wrong, but it was hard to imagine myself doing ordinary stuff with either of them, let alone introducing them to my mates and business colleagues.

So I let it be, for four whole weeks, enjoying what they were willing to give and not pushing it for more. That seemed to work for everybody, and if it never quite made sense that my pleasure always came first, then hey, I was the one getting his cock sucked. Over those four weeks I had them together one more time, with Samara stripping for me while Mirella sucked, Samara twice on her own and Mirella once, always at the weekend but still some of the best sex I've ever had, maybe the best sex, full stop.

It was two months to the day after I'd broken up with Lucie that I got the email. The subject line said "From Lucie, with Love", so I thought she would be trying to get back with me, only the text was just one of those stupid smilies and a link. I clicked on it, expecting some soppy card or something. What I got was a porn sight, garish colours and pictures laid out in a gallery, pictures of Mirella and Samara. I was laughing right away, because I thought it was obvious what had happened and, boy, had she got it wrong. I imagined she thought I'd be ashamed of myself or something, but that only showed how little she knew about men, or so I thought.

I scrolled down a little to look at the first line of pictures and there they were, Samara in her red and white striped top, a black mini-skirt, heels, stocking and a beret, Mirella in a maid's outfit, first dressed, then in a variety of poses, tits on show, bums stuck out to show off their knickers, kissing each other and Samara licking one of Mirella's huge tits. I was actually getting pretty horny for them, and thinking of phoning as soon as I'd sent Lucie a message to tell her her little scheme had failed.

Again I scrolled down, knowing the second line of pictures would be better. They were, first both Mirella and Samara with their tits out and their bums pushed at the camera, about to take down their knickers, again only with their knickers halfway off, showing plenty of lovely rounded bum cheek, and again, with their knickers right down to show it all, only not two hot little virgin pussies, but two sets of dangling ball sacks and two large cocks.

For a few seconds I could only sit there gaping like an idiot as what Lucie had done to me sank in. I'd been tricked with a vengeance, and not just into getting off over two men, but into letting them suck my cock, sucking their tits, even kissing them. To say I was furious just doesn't cut it, and what made it worse was that I'd really got off on it. They'd been the best, and they were men, or shemales anyway, which was they were called on the link, and what made it really bad, for some reason, was that both of them had bigger cocks than I did. Mirella's was bad enough, a great thick brown log of dick with a veiny shaft and a fat head, but Samara's was a monster, jet black, smooth and glossy, and maybe ten inches long erect.

I was going to kill Lucie, and I was going to kill them. Only I wasn't. I couldn't, because to remember what they'd done and to see those two huge cocks and their fat, dark balls was making me feel weak. Besides, it had been good, the best, and there was only one way to rob Lucie of her triumph. So I rang Mirella and suggested they come over for some action.

Looking for love? Our unique dating sites offer the perfect way to meet someone who shares your fantasies.

www.xcitedating.com

Find someone who'll turn fiction into reality and make your fantasies come true.

www.xcitespanking.com

Spanking is our most popular theme – here's the place to find out why!

www.girlfun-dating.co.uk

Lesbian dating for girls who wanna have fun!

www.ultimatecurves.com

For sexy, curvy girls and the men who love them.

Also available at £2.99

Confessions Volume 2

Some experiences just have to be confessed!

There's a knack to getting two girls into bed at the same time. Three simple rules, and one man tells you how ...

A guy whose interest was taboo reveals that he never had trouble recruiting willing female lovers, especially in underground settings ...

Over the knee and on the bare; here's a confession to a lifetime indulging a spanking obsession ...

Even the cruellest of teases eventually offers a taste of the rarest fruit; the trick is to learn how to watch and wait until her desire is ripe ...

ISBN 9781907016325

Also available at £2.99

Confessions Volume 3

Some experiences just have to be
confessed!

Topless girls with attitude and icecream
equals a lot of messy fun for one man
who dares to do more than dream ...
A raid on a fetish club does nothing but
increase the voltage of the sexual
energy coursing through the bad girls ...
In the great outdoors, when you happen
across female strangers misbehaving,
watching can be far more exciting than
joining in ...
The appetites of the wives of powerful
men cannot be underestimated, nor can
the delights of satisfying their hunger ...

ISBN 9781907016332

For more information and great offers
please visit
www.xcitebooks.com